This book belongs to:

....

....

....

Ballet
Stories

Written by Jan Astley, Becky Brookes,
Gaby Goldsack, Kath Jewitt,
Sue Nicholson, Ronne Randall
and Louisa Somerville

Illustrated by Leighton Noyes

Designed by Blue Sunflower Creative

First published by Parragon in 2007
Parragon
Queen Street House
4 Queen Street
Bath BA1 1HE, UK

ISBN 978-1-4054-7624-9

Printed in England

Ballet
Stories

PaRragon
Bath · New York · Singapore · Hong Kong · Cologne · Delhi · Melbourne

Contents

The
Music Box

Laura Brookes picked up an empty cardboard box from the boot of the car and sighed. She was helping her mum and dad move her grandma Millie's belongings into a bungalow. They had just arrived at her grandma's old house to sort everything into cardboard boxes for the move.

"Cheer up, Laura. It will be fun to see what your grandma has been storing away all these years," said her mum, carrying an empty box up the driveway.

Laura loved her grandma very much, but she didn't particularly like cleaning her own bedroom, never mind a whole house full of really old things that probably wouldn't be very interesting.

Laura imagined that all her friends were doing something far more exciting, like going ice-skating or swimming.

"Come on, Laura," said her dad, opening the front door. "The sooner we get started..."

"...I know, the sooner we'll be finished," Laura muttered to herself.

"Right, we'll begin upstairs, I think," said her mum, once they were all inside. "Laura, why don't we go through the things in Grandma's spare room, while Dad sorts out the kitchen?"

Laura began to feel a few butterflies in her tummy. Laura couldn't remember ever being in her grandma's spare room before and wondered what it would be like. She had always wanted to go in the attic too, which was just above her grandma's room, but she had never been allowed because the floorboards weren't very safe.

As her mum opened the door to Grandma's spare room, sunlight poured in through the windows, lighting up the flecks of dust in the air. The room looked magical.

Laura gasped as she looked around the room. Most of the things appeared as if they belonged in some sort of antique shop.

"Wow, I love the dressing table," Laura exclaimed. It was all white, with fancy, curvy legs at the corners and pretty patterned silver handles on the two drawers at the front.

"Your grandma Millie bought that from a little furniture shop in Paris," her mum replied, following Laura's eye. "She was touring there with the ballet company."

"Was Grandma a real ballet dancer, then?" asked Laura, her eyes widening in surprise.

"Oh, yes. She danced in some well-known ballet productions," her mum smiled.

"Wow!" Laura thought. She knew Grandma had danced but she had never realized her grandma had been in shows!

Then, Laura noticed some framed photos at the end of the dressing table. Laura stepped forward to take a closer look. The photos were of Laura dancing in various ballet shows of her own. Laura began to feel a bit bad about grumbling to help with the move. Her grandma was clearly very proud of her.

"Oh, no! I've forgotten the bin-liners," Mum groaned suddenly. "I'll just go and grab a handful from the car. I'll be back in a minute." As soon as her mum was out of the room, Laura noticed something sparkle on the dressing table, beside the mirror.

Laura picked it up carefully.

"It's a silver key," she muttered to herself. "But what was it for?"

"Do you know anything about this?" Laura asked Mum, when she came back upstairs.

Laura's mum carefully took the key from her.

"Yes, yes of course," she smiled, remembering. "It's the key to your grandma's old music box. I had forgotten all about it. She used to wind it up all the time when I was little. Goodness knows where it is now though. Maybe we'll find it later." Laura hoped so. She loved music boxes.

Laura carefully popped the key in her jeans pocket and helped her mum sort through the rest of Grandma's belongings. Soon, everything apart from the bed, wardrobe and dressing table was packed away in bin-liners and boxes. But there was no sign of the music box.

Exhausted, Laura and her parents decided to break for lunch, and eat the sandwiches Laura's mum had prepared earlier that day.

Laura's thoughts turned back to the attic upstairs.

"Mum," she began, after she had swallowed a mouthful of food, "please can I go up and sort through Grandma's things in the attic next?"

Laura's mum looked a bit worried.

"Well, I don't know. Your grandma always said the floorboards weren't very safe. What do you think, Ed?" she asked Laura's dad.

"I'll have a quick look first," her dad replied. "If it's okay I'll let you know."

So, after lunch, Laura's dad went up to the attic. It seemed like he was up there for ages and Laura wished with all of her might that he wouldn't find anything wrong with it.

"The attic seems fine to me," her dad said finally, when he returned to the kitchen. "There's a few bits and bobs up there and it's a bit dirty so be careful where you step."

"Great! Thanks, Dad," Laura beamed excitedly.

She picked up a small cardboard box, and raced up the narrow staircase leading to the attic.

At the top of the stairs, Laura turned the door handle and peered inside. She was surprised to find that there wasn't much in there: just a roll of old carpet, a sewing machine and some flowery-patterned garden chairs.

Suddenly, Laura's attention was drawn to a small pocket of sunlight beaming down from the skylight in the roof. As in her grandma's spare room, the dust seemed to sparkle magically.

Laura placed the cardboard box by the side of the door and moved closer to the light. She noticed that something was tucked away in a corner, covered in lots of cobwebs and dust. As she walked carefully towards it she could see that it was a box with a silver clasp on the front.

"It must have been the clasp that I saw sparkle," thought Laura.

Laura then brushed away the cobwebs and opened the lid. Inside, Laura could see that there was a pretty purple velvet box with a pair of tiny, silver ballet slippers on the front of the box.

"Grandma Millie's music box!" Laura gasped in delight. A tiny, rather tatty ballerina doll stood inside.

Laura took the key from her pocket and put it in the small hole at the side of the box. It fitted perfectly. She began to wind the key round and round. It took a while, as the key was very stiff, but soon a tinkly tune started to play. The little ballerina doll twirled around with short sharp movements.

"Ouch! Eet iz too fast," the ballerina doll seemed to groan in a funny accent. But Laura thought she must have imagined it.

"Silly me," Laura chuckled, "it's just the creaking noise of the music."

But then the ballerina moaned again.

"Pleeez go slower. I 'ave been locked away in zis box for an age!" she grumbled.

Laura couldn't believe it. The ballerina doll was talking!

"Wh-who are you?" she asked cautiously. But, before the ballerina said anything else, the music stopped and the ballerina froze, mid-twirl.

"Oh, that's a shame," thought Laura sadly. She wound the key round again, for longer this time, hoping that the ballerina doll would come to life. Instantly, the music began to play and the ballerina stiffly whirled around once more.

"Zat iz better," sighed the ballerina, when she began to move more smoothly. "Eet feels zo good to be danzin' again."

"So you are real!" Laura grinned at the doll. "I thought I'd imagined you. I'm Laura, by the way."

The ballerina smiled at Laura. It was a bit difficult, though, because she kept twirling around and facing the other way.

"I'm Marie," she replied. "Zank you very much for finding me. I thought I would never danz again. I 'ave been zo lonely in zee box," Marie sniffed.

"Oh, I'm very sorry to hear that," Laura said sympathetically. "Why have you been up here?"

"I don't really know. One day I was talking to Millicent in her room, zen the next day, some men brought me up here and I haven't zeen her zince," Marie replied sadly.

"Who is Millicent?" asked Laura.

"Millicent iz in zee bottom of zis box," said Marie.

Laura was half-expecting to find another talking doll in the music box but, when she peered inside, she couldn't believe what she saw.

There were five old black-and-white photographs of the most beautiful ballerina

Laura had ever seen and a programme with a photo and a caption underneath reading: "Millicent Richards gives her greatest performance ever as the swan in *Swan Lake*."

"Are all these other photos also of Millicent?" Laura whispered excitedly.

"Oui," Marie replied. "Zat iz her."

Laura had loads of questions burning inside her. For a start: Who was Millicent? And what were her photos doing in her grandma's music box? Why had her grandma hidden the music box, and did she know about the talking ballerina? Laura couldn't wait to ask her grandma all these questions when she saw her tomorrow.

Laura carefully shut the music box, promising Marie that she would open it again very soon.

The following morning, Laura and her parents went to Grandma Millie's new bungalow. While her parents unloaded her grandma's things from the car, Laura hurried inside to find her grandma.

"Grandma Millie, I've got something to show you," she said, when she found her in the sitting room. Laura held out the purple velvet box in both hands.

"My music box!" her grandma gasped in surprise, carefully taking it from her granddaughter.

"It was in the attic!" Laura exclaimed impatiently. "Grandma, why did you hide it there? Who's Millicent Richards? And why didn't you tell me you were in shows? And did you know the ballerina doll can talk...?"

"Slow down," her grandma chuckled.

"One thing at a time. The music box was very special to me. I had it given to me as a present for being in a ballet show when I was in France. As I was always moving from place to place I didn't want the box to get damaged, so I put it in a safe place. But then your grandad and I moved to our house and the box was lost. The removal men must have put it in the attic. I kept looking for it but never found it."

"My memory isn't as good as it used to be," her grandma continued, "and I forgot about it after a while."

"Oh!" said Laura. "But why are there photos of someone called Millicent Richards in the music box?"

"The pictures are of me," her grandma chuckled. "I'm Millicent. Millie is short for Millicent and my surname was Richards before I married your grandpa."

"You were the beautiful ballerina in

the photos!" Laura gasped. "Is that you on the front of the programme in the box?" she asked.

"Yes, I was the swan in *Swan Lake*."

"But Grandma, you never said you were a prima ballerina!" said Laura excitedly. "So, you know about the ballerina doll being real too?"

"Oh, I wouldn't say that," her grandma smiled. "But I used to talk to her and, as the music always sounded a bit creaky, it often seemed as if she was speaking."

Laura was disappointed. Maybe she had imagined the ballerina doll too.

"Now, will you do something for me?" Laura's grandma asked her. "Will you keep the music box safe? I have nowhere to put it here, you see. Promise me you'll look after little Marie."

Laura looked up at her grandma in shock. She hadn't mentioned the ballerina doll's name before! How could Grandma have known that?

Just then Laura's parents walked in with a couple of boxes.

"All done, Mum," said Laura's mum. "Everything is unpacked now. We just need you to make sure there isn't anything you wanted to keep in these boxes."

"Will do," Laura's grandma smiled.

Then she turned to wink at Laura and said, "Well? You do promise, don't you?"

Laura thought about the ballerina in the music box and smiled.

"I promise," she whispered.

Sophie's Special Gift

Sophie shifted restlessly in her seat at the City Theatre. She was so happy and excited! Mum had brought her and her best friend, Amy, to see the Starlight Ballet perform. Tonight it was *Cinderella*, and Sophie and Amy could hardly wait for it to begin.

Sophie loved the ballet. Most of all, she loved watching Alicia Harrison dance. Alicia was the Starlight Ballet's prima ballerina, and she was so elegant and graceful that, when she danced, Sophie wanted to dance too. In fact, Sophie's deepest wish was to be just like Alicia Harrison when she grew up.

As the lights went down and the

curtains parted, Sophie turned to Amy and smiled. For the next two hours, they were both transported to a magical, fairy-tale world, where Alicia Harrison went from being a ragged kitchen maid to being the most beautiful, most exquisite dancer at the ball – and the happy bride of the handsome prince.

As she left the theatre, Sophie knew that she would spend the night dreaming of dancing across the stage just as Alicia Harrison had.

The next morning, Sophie and Amy were at their ballet class at Miss Marsh's Academy of Dance, as they were every Saturday morning. As the girls practised their pliés at the barre, Miss Marsh called the class to attention.

"I have a special announcement," she said. "Next week we will have some special visitors. I can't tell you who they are…"

An excited murmur went round the ballet class.

"…but they will want to watch you all dance. So today we must prepare especially well for that performance."

All week, Sophie and Amy tried to guess who the visitors might be.

"Maybe all our parents are coming to surprise us," suggested Sophie as they walked to school together.

"That wouldn't be so special," said Amy. "Our parents have seen us dance loads of times!"

"I know!" said Sophie suddenly, during a skipping game at playtime. "It's the Queen! I'm sure it is!"

"I'll bet it's a famous film star, or someone from TV," added Amy.

"Or someone really cool," said Sophie dreamily, gazing up at a poster of her favourite pop star.

When Saturday came, the girls were no closer to knowing who the mystery visitors might be. They arrived at their ballet class full of anticipation.

Imagine their disappointment when they saw that the visitors were just an ordinary-looking man and woman. They felt very let-down as they changed into their practice clothes.

"Our parents would have been a better surprise," sighed Amy, but they changed their minds when Miss Marsh introduced the man and woman.

"Class, may I present Mr Thomas Wilder, choreographer of the Starlight

Ballet Company…" she paused ever so slightly "…and Miss Alicia Harrison, the prima ballerina."

Sophie and Amy looked at each other and gasped in amazement.

"I can't believe she's really here," whispered Sophie, almost too delighted to speak.

"Wow!" Amy replied. "She looks so different in ordinary clothes and without her hair and make-up done!"

"But she's still really wonderful," sighed Sophie.

Mr Wilder walked to the front of the ballet class.

"Now, I know you're all wondering why we've come to see you today," he said. "Well, this Christmas, as always, the Starlight Ballet Company will be putting on a performance of *The Nutcracker*. And, as always, Miss Harrison will be dancing the role of the Sugar Plum Fairy."

Alicia grinned and did an exaggerated curtsy. The children all laughed.

"As you probably know," Mr Wilder went on, "there are lots of children in *The Nutcracker*, too. This year, we would like five of those children to come from this very class."

"Wicked!" Amy gasped. Sophie could hardly believe her ears.

Mr Wilder then explained that he and Alicia would be watching the children go through their normal class routine, and then would ask seven or eight of them to dance individually. Five of those would be chosen as the lucky ones to dance in *The Nutcracker*.

All the children worked hard as Miss Marsh took them through their set exercises and routines. Meanwhile, Mr Wilder and Alicia stood at the side of the room, watching them all carefully. Sometimes they made notes, and every now and then they would whisper something to each other.

Sophie tried to pretend that they weren't there, because every time she thought about Alicia Harrison watching her she got nervous flutters in her tummy and couldn't concentrate on her movements. Instead, she tried to think about the ballet she and Amy had seen the week before, and imagined herself as Cinderella, gracefully gliding across the ballroom.

When the first part of the class was over, the children took a break while Mr Wilder, Alicia and Miss Marsh talked quietly together next to the piano. The children were all a-buzz, eager to know who would be chosen to dance individually.

At last they were ready. Alicia stood in front of the room and read out the names of three boys and four girls – including Amy and Sophie!

"Well done, all of you," said Miss Marsh, smiling. "Now, even though not everyone has gone through, you all did your best, and I'm very proud of you." Then she asked the children who had been selected to come to the front, while the rest of the class watched from the back.

"Let's begin," Miss Marsh said, with a nod to the pianist.

Sophie stood, as patiently as she could, and watched everyone else as Miss Marsh guided them through routines they had learned in class over the past term.

At last it was her turn to dance. Her insides felt wobbly as she performed her routine, but she kept smiling, remembering what Miss Marsh had taught everyone about expression and attitude.

It was all going really well, until…

"Arabesque," said Miss Marsh.

The arabesque was a difficult pose. Sophie raised her arms gracefully. Then she leaned forward, raised her right leg and…THUD! Sophie tumbled to the floor.

At first there was just silence. Then there were a couple of stifled giggles.

Sophie didn't hear any more, because she fled from the room, her face burning with shame. Amy rushed out after her.

As Sophie bolted into the changing room, she burst into a great flood of miserable tears. Amy was trying to comfort her when they heard a knock on the door.

"Go away!" moaned Sophie.

But there was another gentle knock, and then the door opened just a tiny crack. "Please let me come in," said a soft voice – Alicia Harrison's voice!

"Okay," whispered Sophie.

Alicia sat down on the floor right beside Sophie, "I know exactly how you feel right now," she said kindly.

"How can you?" asked Sophie in tears.

"I can," said Alicia, "because exactly the same thing happened to me when I auditioned for the Starlight Ballet."

"Really?" said Sophie looking up.

"Yes," said Alicia. "As I did an arabesque, I tumbled right over, and I felt as if I wanted the world to end right then and there. But do you know what I did?"

"What?" asked Sophie.

"I got right back up and kept on dancing," said Alicia. "And I still got the place in the company."

Sophie and Amy both smiled.

"Every dancer makes a mistake now and then," Alicia went on, "and accidents happen to all of us. The important thing is to get right back on your feet and keep dancing – and to give it your best effort, no matter what."

Sophie nodded, and so did Amy. And, when Alicia asked if Sophie wanted to try again, she said "Yes". The second time around, remembering Alicia's words, Sophie's dancing was better than ever – with no mishaps, mistakes or accidents at all.

Finally it was time for Alicia and Mr Wilder to announce whom they'd chosen to be in *The Nutcracker*. Everyone in the class held their breath in anticipation as Alicia read out the names:

"Peter, Kate, Tom, Amy and, er...Sophie."

Everyone, including Alicia burst into

applause.
Sophie was
so happy she
thought her
heart would burst.

Sophie and Amy
spent the next few weeks
rehearsing with Alicia
and the Starlight Ballet
Company. They learned all
about what goes on behind the scenes at a
theatre, and what it feels like to dance on a
real stage.

Sophie was more certain than ever
that she wanted to be a real ballerina when
she grew up. She learned from some of the
older dancers how much hard work it
would take, but she knew she wouldn't let
that stop her.

The opening night of *The Nutcracker*
was the most thrilling night of Sophie's life.

The girls' dressing room backstage was a flurry of pink tights, net skirts, sparkly costumes, hair ribbons, shoe ribbons and pots of make-up.

Sophie and Amy were giggling nervously and helping each other with their costumes when there was a knock on the door. It was Ellie, a backstage assistant.

"Is Sophie Warren here?" she asked.

Sophie felt her heart begin to thump.

"Yes," she said.

"Miss Harrison's asked you to come to her dressing room," said Ellie. "Follow me."

As Sophie followed Ellie to Alicia Harrison's private dressing room, she felt very honoured – and very nervous. Why did Alicia want to see her now?

"Hi, Sophie," said Alicia with a warm smile. "Come in." Sophie stepped inside, smelling the lovely scent of roses and lilies – the dressing room was filled with bouquets and cards from Alicia's family, friends and fans.

"I wanted to wish you good luck tonight," Alicia said to Sophie, "though I don't think you need it. You're a very gifted young dancer, and I know you have a wonderful future ahead of you."

"Thank you," murmured Sophie, her eyes shining.

"But I did want to give you something special," Alicia said. "My first performance onstage was in *The Nutcracker*, too, when I was just about your age. And, that night, I wore this ribbon in my hair."

She took a blue velvet hair ribbon out of her dressing-table drawer. It matched Sophie's costume perfectly.

"I'd like you to have it," said Alicia. "Shall I fasten it in your hair for you?"

"Oh, yes, please, Miss Harrison," Sophie breathed. "Thank you so much!"

Sophie danced splendidly that evening. She couldn't see her mum or dad in the audience, but she knew they were there, and she felt so proud to be dancing for them.

Later, she and Amy watched from the wings as Alicia Harrison danced the Sugar Plum Fairy's beautiful pas de deux with the Nutcracker Prince. Sophie sighed with delight and thought again of how much she wanted to be just like Alicia when she grew up. It was her dream – and now, as she touched the blue velvet ribbon in her hair, she knew that she could make it come true.

The Show Must Go On

"Come to the ballet! Saturday night!" Grace called out. She was shivering on the steps of the community hall with a stack of leaflets in her hand. Miss Briggs, the ballet mistress, had told her to wear her ballet costume to attract attention. But Grace was freezing. She couldn't wait to get rid of her pile of leaflets!

"Please take one!" she said to passers-by. "And please come to our production of *The Sleeping Beauty*!" A few people took the leaflets. Some stuffed them straight in their bags, but others began to read them. Then people started to nudge each other and somebody stifled a giggle. Grace didn't know what all the fuss was about.

"I know it's only a fairytale," she began. "But it's a wonderful ballet…" Her voice trailed off, as a couple of boys shrieked with laughter and began doing robot impressions. A woman with a child in a pram was wiping tears of laughter from her eyes. "Whatever is the matter with everyone?" thought Grace. "Why is *The Sleeping Beauty* so funny?" A man stepped forward and pointed at the top of the leaflet with his finger.

"I'm sorry, young lady," he said, "but it is rather amusing." Grace stared at the first line. There, in huge letters that Grace had printed herself, she read:

THE BLEEPING BEAUTY

"Oh, no," she groaned.

It was the start of a bad few days. At home that night, Grace read the story of *The Sleeping Beauty* to her little brother Joey. She told him how the bad fairy cast a spell on the baby princess at her christening, and how, 16 years later, the princess pricked her finger on a poisoned needle and fell asleep for one hundred years.

"Why didn't she die?" Joey interrupted. Grace reminded him that Lilac, the good fairy, had changed the bad fairy's spell to make it less harmful.

"Anyway, if Sleeping Beauty died, then the Prince wouldn't be able to wake her with a kiss," Grace explained, snapping the book shut. Joey slid down under the blankets and mumbled.

"Well, I don't want to come to your stupid ballet, anyway!"

The next day, the ballet class had such a disastrous rehearsal that Miss Briggs threatened to resign. Grace sat on a chair in the community hall, waiting to practise her part as Sleeping Beauty, the best role in the whole ballet. She was watching the others rehearse the part where the good fairies arrive at the baby princess's christening. Instead of flitting lightly around the royal cot in perfect formation, these flat-footed fairies stampeded across the floor as if they might well trample on the baby!

One fairy tripped over another one's feet and they both came crashing to the floor. Miss Briggs clutched her forehead and closed her eyes.

"The baby's christening is supposed to be attended by FAIRIES, not WINGED ELEPHANTS!" she boomed. The fairies stood in a line and stared at their toes. "Repeat!" snapped Miss Briggs. "And please dance in time to the music! Thank you, Mr Stebbings. And one, and two…!"

Mr Stebbings the pianist, who was rather afraid of Miss Briggs, nervously struck up the chords and the fairies began to dance. Grace swung her legs back and forth. "Nearly time for my part," she thought excitedly.

"Come along, Grace! You're up next," Miss Briggs was calling.

"Yes, Miss Br…atchoo!" Grace sneezed violently. Miss Briggs arched an eyebrow.

"Have you got a cold?" she asked Grace frostily.

"Oh, no, I don't think so. I expect it's just dust," Grace replied weakly. "I've been cleaning my room…atchoo!"

"Because if you have," Miss Briggs continued, ice cubes shattering in her voice, "I shall have to send you home! I can't risk the entire cast's health, can I?"

"No, Miss Briggs," replied Grace forlornly. She didn't dare remind her that it had been Miss Briggs' idea for her to stand on the street in winter wearing a tutu!

Grace blew her nose and started to dance. She danced the scene of the ball to celebrate Sleeping Beauty's sixteenth birthday, the section where she receives a bunch of flowers in which the poisoned needle is hidden. She pretended to prick herself on an imaginary needle. Then, instead of floating gracefully to the floor to sleep for a hundred years, Grace sneezed loudly again.

"Stop! Stop!" shouted Miss Briggs, clapping her hands briskly. "Go home, Grace, and get better!" Mr Stebbings looked as though he might say something in Grace's defence but Miss Briggs glared at him and he fiddled with his tie instead. Grace went home and climbed into bed. It couldn't get any worse...could it?

The next day, Grace felt much better and her cold had gone. Then she remembered: it was the day of the dress rehearsal! She leapt out of bed, grabbed her costumes and ran to the community hall.

The rehearsal was about to start and Miss Briggs was already in a bad mood. Then Grace saw why she was angry.

"You've had all this time," Miss Briggs was saying, "and still your costumes aren't finished!" Indeed, there were some very strange sights. One of the fairies was dressed in blue, while all the others wore pink. Instead of a golden crown, the king sported a paper hat from a Christmas cracker that fell over his eyes. And, as for Tom, who was playing the handsome prince…he had forgotten his costume so was resigned to wearing his school uniform.

Grace's friend Bonnie, who was dancing the part of Lilac, the good fairy, had brought her little dog with her.

"Sit quietly, Scruff. There's a good boy," Bonnie whispered, as she tried to settle him down at the side of the stage.

The rehearsal began. At first, all seemed to go quite well. But then it was time for the good fairy and the bad fairy to confront each other. Closer and closer they danced and then, just as the bad fairy raised her arm to pretend to swipe at the good one, Scruff the dog ran out to defend his mistress.

"No, Scruff!" shouted Bonnie, as he shot across the stage, teeth bared and growling. The bad fairy sprang out of the way, clutched at a piece of scenery to stop herself falling and brought the whole cardboard palace crashing to the floor.

Miss Briggs looked as if she was about to explode as Scruff sat centre stage wagging his little tail, until Bonnie dragged him off. The scenery was reassembled and the rehearsal continued. Things seemed to be going a bit better until the scene in the castle, when the whole court is put under the bad fairy's spell. The cast pretended to fall into a deep sleep…except that one child really did fall asleep and began to snore loudly!

Now they were reaching the end of the rehearsal and Grace was feeling pleased with herself. She had danced well – and she hadn't sneezed once. It was the final scene, in which she dances at her wedding to the prince.

The whole cast was on the stage, dancing the parts of the guests at the wedding. There were other fairytale characters, such as Red Riding Hood and Puss in Boots. ("Puss in Trainers!" Miss Briggs had barked at yet another incomplete costume.)

Round and round they twirled, Grace

in her beautiful gown and Tom, the prince, in his school uniform. Then, just at the end, on the final pirouette, Tom lifted his arm to leap and...fell, smacking Grace on his way down.

"Oh, no!" she thought. She was lying on the floor with Miss Briggs' face looking anxiously down into hers. In fact, Grace realized that the entire cast was standing over her with expressions of horror. Grace was aware that her face hurt. In fact, it was throbbing! She reached with her fingers to where it felt sore, on her cheek below her eye.

"Ahhh!" she winced, as Miss Briggs clamped a piece of ice wrapped in a tea towel to her cheek.

"I just hope you don't get a black eye. We can't have Sleeping Beauty with a black eye," Miss Briggs was groaning. Grace sat up slowly.

"Ooh, my face is sore. What just

happened?" she asked, puzzled.

"It was me," sighed Tom. "My elbow…well, it caught you on the cheek. I'm so sorry, Grace," he added.

When Grace got home, her mum stared at her in dismay. Grace went into the bathroom and looked at her face in the mirror. Her cheek was pink and swollen and already beginning to turn a nasty shade of blue. She could see Joey's face dancing up and down behind hers, grinning and giggling. He was holding up a book and pointing to a picture of a blue-faced ape.

"Monkey face!" he cried. Grace buried her face in her mum's arm.

"What will I do?" she wailed. "I can't perform tomorrow looking like this!"

"Don't worry," Mum replied. "I'll think of something."

Grace went to her room and locked the door. She lay on her bed with her face on the pillow and wept. "Why me?" she thought sadly. Then she fell asleep, exhausted. Some time later, she woke up and heard her mum talking on the telephone. Grace strained her ears.

"Yes," said her mum. "Oh, thank you. That's wonderful. See you tomorrow. Goodbye." There was a knock at the bedroom door.

"Can I come in, Grace?" came her mum's voice. Grace unlocked the door and her mum came over to hug her.

"I phoned my friend Beth. She used to dance," her mum explained.

"And?" asked Grace, puzzled.

"And she said she'd see what she could do. She's coming here before the show. We'll just have to see. I don't want to get your hopes up," Mum continued, "but she says she's got some ideas on what to do."

It was all very mysterious and her mum wasn't sure what her friend Beth had in mind. Grace would just have to wait.

The next day, the bruise was worse, with all the colours of the rainbow in it. Joey found it all very amusing, much to Grace's annoyance.

"It's a real shiner," the postman called, seeing Grace's anxious face at the window, as she waited for Beth.

Just when Grace was sure that she wasn't coming, there was a knock at the door and there stood a neat little woman, who reminded Grace of Miss Briggs, except that she was a lot more smiley. She had an awful lot of bags and boxes with her.

"Hello, I'm Beth," she said, "and you must be Grace! Now let's have a proper look at you."

Grace sat on a chair and Beth looked at her face. It was rather like being at the doctor's, Grace thought. Beth examined Grace's bruise and muttered a few things under her breath. What was she thinking? Was it an impossible task? Finally, she smiled and said:

"I'm going to make you look beautiful, Grace, and no one will know about your accident. I've seen far worse than this. Always remember the dancer's moto: 'The show must go on!'"

It turned out that Beth had taught make-up to many famous ballet dancers.

"How come you don't dance any more?" Grace asked Beth. Beth chuckled before answering.

"Well, to be honest, I wasn't very good.

I'm not very graceful and was always tripping over and losing my balance. I love everything about ballet: the costumes, the shows, the music. Doing make-up for the ballerinas means I can still be involved with the shows. Now then, let's start on you shall we."

Beth then began to make up Grace's face and, while she did so, she told Grace that all ballet dancers do their own stage make-up. She was full of funny stories about dancers who'd put on too much rouge, or who had made themselves up as a warty witch, when they should have been a princess. Grace watched in fascination as Beth's brush flew around, mixing colours, dabbing and wiping. It was like watching a painter at work!

She noticed Joey's face at the door. He was now watching intently and not laughing at her.

"I want a bruise too!" he whispered to his mum. At last, Beth had finished her work and held up a mirror for Grace to see.

"Wow!" Grace gasped. It was incredible. As if by magic, the bruise had vanished! "Thank you!" she exclaimed.

"It's my pleasure," replied Beth, laughing. "May I come and watch the show tonight?"

"Oh yes, please!" exclaimed Grace. "I must get changed into my first costume now." Soon she was standing at the door, wearing the Sleeping Beauty costume that her mum had made for her.

"I have a present for you," said Beth, "because you were so good. You wouldn't believe some of the tantrums I've dealt with over the years!" She held out a small wrapped package.

Grace opened it and inside was a beautiful, soft brush.

"It's a proper stage make-up brush," said Beth. "Look after it and it will last you all your dancing life."

"Oh, I will!" said Grace.

"Let's go, or we'll be late," said her mum. "Are you coming, Joey?"

"You bet," he said. So Mum, Joey and Beth sat in the front row of the community hall waiting for the show to begin.

This time all the fairies looked pretty, and danced properly. Scruff was nowhere to be seen, and Tom danced brilliantly as the prince. Best of all, Grace danced better than she had ever done in her life, and nobody could see that she had a black eye.

After that, she never forgot Beth's motto…and, next time you have a bad day, make sure you remember it too!

Ballet Lessons for Lily

L ily loved ballet. She was the star pupil at Bickley Academy of Dance. She had passed lots of exams and her ballet teacher said she had real talent.

Lily had just landed the starring role of Clara in the Easter production of *The Nutcracker*, when her dad made an announcement.

"I've got a new job in the country," he told Lily and her brother, Bill. "I'm going to be managing an orchard in a small village called Mereton. The job comes with a house so we'll be moving in two weeks time."

"But that's before the ballet school's Easter production," gasped Lily. "Will I be able to come back to play Clara?"

"I'm afraid not," said Dad, shaking his head sadly. "Mereton is a long way away."

Lily felt very sad but she knew that Mum and Dad had always dreamed about moving to the country, so she tried her best to be cheerful. She might not be able to play Clara, but she was sure she would be able to continue her ballet lessons in Mereton.

Two weeks later, Lily and her family were settled in their new home. Mum, Dad and Bill thought it was great. They had an enormous garden and Dad had already agreed that Bill could keep chickens. Lily thought the house and garden were pretty cool too.

When she and Bill visited the village school, they both agreed that it looked much nicer than their old one. Lily was really looking forward to going there after the Easter holidays. She had even met a girl from down the lane, who was going to be in the same class as her. Her name was Gemma and she and Lily were already the best of friends.

There was only one thing that Lily wasn't happy about. There was no ballet school in the village, or even in the surrounding villages. Mum had promised to take her to a big dance school in town once a month, but Lily knew that it wouldn't be enough. Without regular lessons she wouldn't get any better and she wouldn't be able to pass any more exams.

Gemma and Bill tried to persuade Lily that there were lots of other things to do instead of ballet.

"Riding's fun," said Gemma, who owned a pony of her own. "I wouldn't mind trying it," said Lily, as she pirouetted around the garden. "But it's just not ballet."

"Well, how about football?" suggested

Bill, who was kicking his ball against the garden fence.

"Don't do that," gasped Gemma. "The old bat who lives next door will yell at you."

"What old bat?" asked Lily. "I haven't seen anyone next door."

Gemma shuddered. "Miss Grill," she whispered, creeping over to the garden fence and pointing a shaky finger at the bungalow next door.

"She only ever comes out to shout at us for kicking balls into her garden or making too much noise. She even has her groceries delivered. Some people say..." at which point Gemma paused and looked around to make sure nobody was listening, "...that she's a witch – and they could be right. She's tall and thin and wears her hair scraped back in a bun. She walks with a limp and has a black cat. Watch out for her. She hates children!"

Lily shuddered as she remembered seeing a black cat walking along the fence that very morning. He had hissed and arched his back when Lily had called out to him. She also remembered having a feeling that she was being watched while she practised her ballet positions in the garden one afternoon.

The next day, Lily and Bill were playing catch in the garden when Bill threw the ball too hard and it shot into the garden next door. Lily looked at Bill with huge eyes. "What should we do?" she asked. "Should we knock on her door and ask for it back?"

"Not likely," hissed Bill. "You heard what Gemma said. She's a kid-hating witch. Let's just leave it there."

"No way," said Lily. "You go and get it."

"I'm not getting it," cried Bill. "You go and get it if you want it so much. But I bet you won't, because you're nothing but a big chicken."

Lily frowned as Bill began to cluck loudly and strut around like a chicken. No one called her 'chicken'.

"Right," she whispered, "I'll show you." Lily climbed up the apple tree that grew beside the fence and dropped down on the other side. She looked around quickly but couldn't see the ball anywhere.

She turned back to the fence and whistled to get Bill's attention.

"I can't see it," she whispered. "I'm going to look around."

As she twirled back round she bumped into something soft that hadn't been there before.

"Are you looking for this?" asked a voice.

Lily looked up. There was a tall, thin lady with a bun. She knew straight away that it must be Miss Grill – the kid-hating witch! As Lily tried to step back she found the fence blocking her way. There was no escape. She looked wildly around, and then froze. A black cat was wrapping itself around the lady's leg. And, even worse, the lady was holding a broomstick in one hand. She really was a witch! Lily closed her eyes and waited for something to happen. Maybe the witch would turn her into a

toad, but nothing happened, until the lady
began to speak once more.

"Are you looking for this?" she repeated.

Lily opened one eye and peeped out.
The lady was holding Bill's football in
her hand.

"Y...y...yes," stuttered
Lily. "T...t...that's all I
want. I didn't mean any
harm. Please don't cast
a spell on me." Lily was
amazed when the lady
chuckled. It didn't
sound anything like a
witchy cackle. Lily
opened both her eyes
and took a good look at
the witch.

Lily decided to
chance a closer inspection. Her old
neighbour didn't look at all like a witch.

In fact, she was young and pretty. And the broomstick she was holding wasn't a broomstick at all. It was a walking stick.

"Just try to be more careful in future," said the lady, handing Lily the ball. "Balls frighten Kitty. He's a nervous cat and he's scared of noisy children and balls."

"Thank you," said Lily, feeling rather silly. She went to climb back over the fence but the lady stopped her. "Why not use the gate?" she asked.

As the lady led Lily down the garden path, Lily couldn't help noticing that she limped quite badly. She watched her out of the corner of her eye and noticed something else. She was wearing ballet shoes. How strange. Lily just had to say something.

"Why are you wearing ballet shoes?" she asked.

"I've been dancing in the garden," explained the lady. "I love dancing outside.

I do it every day if the weather is good."

"So do I!" cried Lily. Then she looked at the lady's walking stick. "But how do you…" she stopped, not knowing quite what to say next.

"You mean, how do I dance with this limp?" she asked. "Well, I can't dance as well as I used to. But I seem to get by. I really love ballet."

"So do I!" exclaimed Lily. "Would you like to see?"

The lady looked amused as she nodded her head. Lily never needed much encouragement and instantly began to twirl around the garden. After a few seconds, the lady put down her stick and joined her.

Together they spun and twirled, leapt and skipped. They both finished by going up onto the tips of their toes and spinning round in a dramatic arabesque. Lily was amazed to see the lady spin much faster and more expertly than she could.

Lily sank back onto her heels and watched with an open mouth. After what seemed like ages, the lady came to a neat halt and swept Lily a graceful curtsy.

"Wow!" gasped Lily. "You're really good. I've never seen anyone dance like that. Where did you learn to dance?"

The lady limped over to her stick, before answering. "I was a ballerina until I had my accident. I trained at the International School of Ballet and Dance and danced all over the world. But then I slipped and broke my ankle. I've had this silly limp ever since."

"But your limp disappears when you dance," said Lily. "Surely you could be a ballerina again?"

"No, I'm afraid not," said the lady. "My ankle is just not strong enough. Oh, I can dance for a little while, but my ankle soon

starts to ache and I have to stop."

"I'm sorry," said Lily, who could imagine how terrible it must have been to give up a career as a ballerina. She dreamt of being one herself one day. "What do you do now?" she asked.

"Nothing much," laughed the lady. "I don't like people to see me limp around, because I hate people feeling sorry for me. So I stay here most of the time."

"But don't you get lonely?" asked Lily.

"A little," replied the lady. "But I have Kitty to keep me company. And perhaps we could be friends. You will come again, won't you? My name's Amelia, by the way."

"Oh, I'd love to," cried Lily. "Perhaps we could dance again. It's great to find someone else who loves ballet. I used to go to ballet lessons every week but then we moved here and there's nowhere to go."

"I'll tell you what," said Amelia. "Next time you come, I'll teach you some new steps. Would you like that?"

Lily couldn't believe her ears. "Would you really? That would be brilliant! Can I come tomorrow?"

Amelia laughed at Lily's enthusiasm. "I'd like that," she smiled. "But you'd better ask your parents first."

"I will," shouted Lily, as she danced out of the gate and all the way home.

The next day, Lily spent all morning at

Amelia's house. Amelia showed her some new steps and pointed out ways that she could improve those she already knew. When Lily was unsure of how to do something, Amelia would put down her stick and show her how.

"You really are a great teacher," Lily told Amelia. "Would you mind if I brought my friend Gemma round to meet you? She's never done ballet but I'm sure she'd love it if she was shown what to do."

Amelia looked a little unsure. She wasn't used to people coming round. And she wasn't sure she wanted another little girl seeing how badly she limped. But then she looked at Lily's eager face and smiled. "Okay," she said. "Bring her and we'll see how we get along."

So, the next afternoon, Lily arrived with Gemma in tow. Gemma definitely looked the part. Lily had lent her one of her leotards and a pair of ballet shoes that she had outgrown. Amelia started off by showing Gemma the positions. At first Gemma felt a bit silly but before long she began to enjoy herself. And when she saw Lily and Amelia dance together she clapped her hands and jumped up and down excitedly.

"You're fantastic," she cried. "I want to dance like that. Can you show me how?"

Amelia laughed. "It will take a while, but if you come again I'll teach you some more steps."

After that, Lily and Gemma both returned to see Amelia as often as they could. Amelia was such a good teacher, that they both improved enormously.

By the time Lily started her new school, word had got around about their ballet lessons, and all the little girls in the village wanted to have a go. But Lily wasn't

sure. She knew how shy Amelia was about people seeing her limp.

"Let me have a word with her," said her mum, when Lily explained the problem. And later that evening she went around to have a chat. While she was gone, Lily sat at home worrying.

"I do hope she's not cross," Lily said to Bill. "She might decide she doesn't want

Gemma and I to go round any more." But Bill wasn't listening.

"Do you think she'll teach boys to dance?" he asked Lily. "I wouldn't mind having a go but I wouldn't want to wear a girl's tutu."

"You only wear tutus when you perform, silly," and she jokingly tried to put a tutu over his head. Then she heard the front door open. She heard Mum laughing, and then she heard somebody else laugh. It was Amelia.

"Amelia's come round for dinner," explained Mum, leading the visitor into the kitchen. "We're going to chat about the ballet lessons she's going to hold. We reckon she should be able to hire out the village hall."

"Yes," added Amelia. "I think I'll start with a couple of Saturday classes. Then, if that's popular, I could start doing some after-school classes. What do you think, Lily?"

Lily was bursting with joy. She threw herself at Amelia and hugged her round the waist. "I think that sounds brilliant," she cried. "I think you're brilliant." But then Lily thought of something and began biting her lip. "Don't you mind people seeing your limp?" she asked slowly.

"Well, I've decided it's about time I started getting out and about. I've been hiding myself away for far too long. I've got you to thank for making me realize that I shouldn't be so self-conscious."

Lily smiled shyly, and then did a plié. "Do you think we'll have a Christmas performance?" she asked.

"Yes," smiled Amelia.

"Could we please do *The Nutcracker*?" asked Lily.

"Of course," smiled Amelia.

"Could I be Clara?" asked Lily.

"Definitely I can't think of anyone more perfect!" smiled Amelia.

"Brilliant!" laughed Lily. "I know all the steps." And, there and then, she began her very own performance of *The Nutcracker*.

Boys Don't Do Ballet!

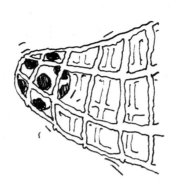

"Jamie," called his sister, Alice, "Rob's on the phone. It's about football." Alice looked at her mother and smiled. Jamie and his football! He thought about nothing else. If Jamie wasn't at home, or at school, there was only one other place he would be – on the football pitch. Jamie was obsessed.

Alice could hear him on the phone talking to Rob.

"Extra practice? When? Tonight, 6.30! Okay, see you there."

"Not more football," teased Alice, when he put the phone down.

"It's better than your stupid ballet," snapped Jamie.

"You can't compare football with

ballet," replied his sister loftily. "Ballet is graceful, beautiful and uplifting. Football is sweaty, muddy and noisy. It's just a load of boys kicking a ball backwards and forwards."

"Ballet is for wimps," said Jamie. "What sort of a man wears tights? I wouldn't be seen dead in them."

"You're not fit enough to do ballet," giggled Alice.

"You've got to be joking," cried Jamie. "Footballers are superfit! You try running as fast as you can for one and a half hours."

"You try lifting a girl above your head," countered Alice.

"No problem," declared Jamie.

"Go on then. Try and lift me," Alice challenged him.

"Stop, you two," laughed Mum. "There's only one way you're going to settle this argument. Alice, you'll have to go to a football match, and, Jamie, you'll have to go to a ballet. Then you'll both know what you are talking about."

"There's no way you'll get me to a ballet," cried Jamie.

"And there's no way I would waste a Saturday afternoon watching a load of boys kicking a ball around a muddy field," cried Alice putting her hands on her hips defiantly.

Jamie and Alice often had this conversation and they always disagreed.

Alice loved ballet. Mum had taken her to see her first ballet when she was very small and she loved it the moment she saw it. After that you couldn't stop Alice from dancing.

She danced around the house. She danced with her friends, and she danced at school. She joined a ballet class and, whenever she could, she watched it on

television. She would have preferred to see it live in a theatre but her family lived in a small village a long way from anywhere. That's why she couldn't believe her luck when she heard at school that the Premiere Dance Company was going to perform a ballet called *Spartacus* in the village hall.

The Premiere Dance Company was famous for touring different countries in Europe. It didn't just visit the big towns and cities but small villages and isolated communities, so that people who didn't normally get the chance to watch a real performance could see it for themselves.

"Mum, we must go," cried Alice, overcome with excitement. "All my friends are going."

"Of course we'll go," smiled Mum. "Jamie," she added, "why don't you come with us?"

"No, thanks," replied Jamie. "My friends would think I was some kind of weirdo if I went to a ballet."

"If you come, I promise I'll watch you play in the championship football match," suggested Alice.

Jamie was quiet. He would have liked Alice to come to the championship. He was good at football and he wanted her to see him play.

"We won't tell your friends," added Alice, sensing his hesitation. "What have you got to lose?"

"Anyway," Mum explained, "*Spartacus* isn't a romantic ballet. It's about Roman soldiers and gladiators."

"I'll think about it," Jamie muttered. He gathered up his kit and went off to play his beloved football.

On the night of the first performance of *Spartacus*, the village hall was packed. Jamie had only agreed to go at the last minute, mainly to stop Alice nagging him. Naturally he hadn't said a word to his friends and now, as he sank down in his seat, he looked round nervously to see if he could see anyone who might give him away.

There were some of Alice's friends close by, but Alice said she would make sure they didn't say anything. The rest of the audience was mainly women and girls. There were very few men. Jamie pulled his baseball cap down over his eyes and kept low in his seat. Luckily the hall wasn't well-lit and soon it would be dark altogether.

It was also quite noisy. There was a small orchestra in front of the raised-up platform at the end of the hall and the players were tuning their instruments. There was a lot of chattering and rustling of programmes and from behind a curtain Jamie could hear the sound of what he supposed were the dancers practising their steps.

Jamie wished he hadn't agreed to come. It was going to be torture. He sank further into his seat and gave a small groan. Alice heard it and gave him a dig in the ribs.

"Shut up, it's going to start," she hissed.

Suddenly the music began. There was a burst of sound as the orchestra played the opening chords of the overture. The audience quietened expectantly and the lights dimmed.

When the curtain rose the stage was empty. Jamie had to admit that even with no action the music itself was pretty impressive. He had never heard so many instruments playing together in such a small space before and the volume of sound seemed to vibrate through the room.

Then, just as he thought the music couldn't possibly get any louder, there was a massive roll of drums and a man dressed as a gladiator ran onto the stage and leapt

high into the air. It was so dramatic the whole audience gasped, including Jamie.

The dancer remained motionless for what seemed like ages, hovering above the stage like a bird in flight. Then, almost as if he was moving in slow motion, he landed and began to spin in circles round and round the stage at a speed so fast it was almost impossible to follow him.

Although the dancer was powerfully built, his movements were graceful and perfectly controlled. Jamie couldn't take his eyes off him. It was like watching a tiger raging through the jungle.

When the dancer had circled the stage twice, he finished dead in the centre and stopped, his arms above his head and his body perfectly still. The only visible sign that he had done anything at all energetic was a slight movement of the chest as his lungs gulped in much-needed air.

The audience rose to its feet, clapping wildly, Jamie amongst them. He couldn't help it. The impact of seeing so brilliant a dancer at such close-quarters left him feeling stunned. It was not what he had expected at all.

For the rest of the ballet Jamie watched and waited for the gladiator to reappear. Each time he appeared on stage, whether it was with a female partner or on his own, he was magnificent. When he took his bow at the end, the whole audience rose to its feet and cheered him to the rafters.

Jamie had never felt so thrilled or so excited before, not even when his football team had reached the final of the schools championship last year. When he got home that night he couldn't stop thinking about what he had seen. He tried to put it out of his head but the excitement of the evening kept returning.

The following night, without saying anything to anyone, Jamie went to see the performance again. He enjoyed it just as much the second time and, when it was finished, he waited by the exit for the dancers to come out. He wanted to tell the male dancer just how good he thought he was.

When all the members of the ballet company came out, Jamie hardly recognized the man he was waiting to see. He was dressed in jeans and trainers and was wearing a baseball cap. The dancer stopped when he saw Jamie. He had noticed him in the audience and wondered why he had come to see the ballet a second time.

"Hi," he said.

"Hi," replied Jamie, feeling really shy.

"You must like ballet a lot to come twice," suggested the dancer.

"No," replied Jamie, "I mean, yes. Actually," he admitted, "this is the first ballet I've ever been to."

"What did you think of it?" asked the dancer.

"I thought you were really great," blurted out Jamie.

"Thanks a lot," the dancer replied, grinning.

"Usually, I only like football," said Jamie.

"I like football too," said the man, "but I wasn't very good at it. I'm better now. Dancing has made me fit and my football has improved. Why don't you give it a try? Dancing, I mean. I know someone who runs a ballet school not far away."

"My friends would think I was a girl if I took ballet lessons," muttered Jamie, and then felt embarrassed for what he'd said.

"Don't tell them," said the dancer. "Do it once a week. Then if you don't like it you can stop. That's what I did when I was about your age."

"Will I have to wear tights and a leotard?" asked Jamie.

"Of course not," laughed the man. "Shorts and a T-shirt, usually."

Jamie thought a lot about what the dancer had said. What harm could it do? As long as nobody ever found out about it. And it would be great to be that fit. He wouldn't mention it to anyone, except perhaps his mum. He would need her to take him and bring him back.

Jamie's mum was all for it and, every Wednesday evening after school, the two of them sneaked out of the house and disappeared for a couple of hours.

"Where are you two off to?" Alice asked once when she saw them getting in the car.

"Jamie's in training for the big match," said Mum quickly. It wasn't really a fib. Jamie was in training. He was training his body to be fitter than it had ever been before.

"Football, football, football," said Alice in a bored voice. "That's all he ever thinks about," and she lifted her hand to her mouth and did a pretend yawn.

Jamie didn't say anything but he smiled to himself. The dancing lessons were beginning to pay off. He could feel himself getting fitter and fitter by the week. He was using muscles he had never used before and he was learning to control his movements just as he had seen the dancer doing at the ballet.

He was also enjoying himself. He knew he could never take up dancing as a professional career – you had to be really dedicated to do that, and the amount of work was tremendous…hours and hours of gruelling practice, aching muscles and sore feet. Every part of the body was exercised until it was as strong as it could possibly be.

Jamie's football was improving too. Now, when he went to head the ball, he was able to leap twice as high in the air as anybody else. When he ran for the ball he was faster than anyone else. And, after two hours of practice, when his friends seemed ready to drop, Jamie seemed like he could go on forever.

"You seem fitter, have you been working out?" his friend Rob asked him, when they were getting changed one evening after practice.

"Sort of," answered Jamie.

"What do you mean, sort of?" asked Rob puzzled.

Jamie took a deep breath and decided to tell his teammates his secret. After all, it had helped him and it could help them –

and that would mean the whole team playing better.

When Jamie told them what he had been doing they thought he was kidding.

"Ballet lessons?" they chorused.

"Prancing about in tights pretending to be a fairy?" they laughed, putting their arms over their heads and skipping around the changing room.

Jamie shook his head. "You've got it all wrong, that's what I thought at first. I know it seems silly," he said, "but ballet is really tough. Honestly, it's the best workout you can have. Look how it's helped me. Why don't you come with me and give it a go?"

His friends stopped prancing about and looked at each other. Then they looked at Jamie. They could see for themselves what good shape he was in.

"It'll be worth it if it helps us to win the championship tournament," Jamie grinned.

The boys agreed because they all wanted to jump as high as Jamie, and keep running for as long as him.

So for the next few weeks, every Wednesday evening, the ballet school was full to overflowing with boys of all shapes and sizes practising their positions at the barre and learning how to leap and twirl without getting out of breath.

In the end it was worth it. When the day of the championship tournament arrived everyone was ready. They ran faster, tackled better and kicked the ball harder to get into the final.

Just when there were two minutes left until the final whistle, Rob passed the ball to Jamie who leapt into the air to head the winning goal into the net.

His team had won! It was the best game they had ever played, thanks to Jamie's winning goal but, more importantly, because they were the fittest team in the whole championship, and all because of ballet.

But the very best thing of all was the fact that Alice was in the crowd, cheering, and discovering that she really liked football after all!

The Late Audition

Sammy and her best friend, Poppy, were ballet-crazy. Their bedroom walls were covered with posters of famous ballerinas and certificates from their ballet exams. Their bookshelves were filled with stories and films about ballet. They even spent all their spare time pretending to be the prima ballerinas in their favourite performances.

Of course, Sammy and Poppy didn't want to just pretend. The two girls dreamed of becoming professional dancers one day.

They had both attended Mrs Brown's ballet class at the village hall for as long as they could remember. Every Saturday afternoon, without fail, they packed their bags with a leotard and ballet shoes, met at the corner, and walked to their ballet class. It was the highlight of the week. And, most evenings after school, they met to practise their ballet exercises. The best friends were ballet-crazy!

But, though Sammy and Poppy loved their classes with Mrs Brown, they knew they would have to win a place at the National School of Ballet if they were ever to become real ballerinas.

One afternoon, Mrs Brown called Sammy and Poppy over at the end of their dance class.

"Well, girls," she smiled. "You did very well today. You are both quite gifted."

Sammy and Poppy blushed with pleasure. "Thank you, Mrs Brown," they both chorused.

"But you realize it's not just about talent," continued Mrs Brown seriously.

"To become a professional dancer, one has to practise continuously."

"We practise just about every night, Mrs Brown," replied Poppy eagerly.

"And that's why I've decided that you are ready for the next stage," replied their teacher. "I'd like you both to audition for a place at the National School of Ballet. You will be dancing for Madame Lemage."

The girls could hardly believe their ears. Madame Lemage was famous in the world of ballet. Once, she was one of the greatest prima ballerinas of her time. Now she was head of the best ballet school in the country.

"Madame Lemage!" gasped Sammy. "Do you think we're good enough?"

Mrs Brown smiled. "I do," she said firmly, "if you put everything you have got into preparing for the audition. Are you ready for the challenge?"

"Oh, yes!" cried Sammy and Poppy in unison. "When can we start?"

From that moment on, the two girls could think of nothing but their audition. Every spare moment was spent preparing for the big day. Three times a week, they had extra classes with Mrs Brown. And, every afternoon after school, they met up to help each other with their audition piece –

a special dance of their own composition, to be performed for Madame Lemage. Poppy had chosen a lively piece of music to dance to, and made up a dance about cats. Sammy had decided on a beautiful floaty piece. Her dance was supposed to represent butterflies.

"I've practised so much, I think I'm doing pirouettes in my sleep," laughed Sammy, as they walked to school one sunny morning.

Poppy grinned. "I know how you feel," she said. "I suddenly realized I was doing leaps in the bus queue the other day. Everyone must have thought I was mad!"

The dates of the auditions finally came through. The two girls opened their envelopes excitedly.

"Monday 25th March at 11am," Poppy read out loud. "What about you?"

Sammy pulled out the letter. "Monday

25th March at 10am," she read. "Great! We can travel up to the auditions on the same train. At least we can both be nervous together!"

As the day of the auditions approached, Sammy and Poppy got more and more excited – and more and more nervous.

"I hope you have thought about what you are going to wear," said Mrs Brown at their final class. "It is most important that you look clean and tidy for your audition. Scruffy old leotards will never do. Madame Lemage is a most elegant lady."

Sammy and Poppy laughed. "We've both got new leotards and wraps," said Poppy. "Sammy's outfit is lilac, and mine is pink. We've even got matching ribbons and hair slides."

"And we're going to help each other put our hair up," added Sammy. "We've been practising new styles."

Mrs Brown nodded approvingly. "I know you girls will make me proud," she smiled. "I'll see you both tomorrow at the train station at 8am sharp. Now, please don't be late."

But, on the morning of the audition, things didn't go quite as planned. Poppy was at the station at 8am, as arranged. But, though Sammy was up early and ready to leave on time, her mum's car wouldn't start.

"We're going to miss the train," wailed Sammy, pacing up and down the driveway. "What are we going to do?"

Poppy waited anxiously at the station barrier for Sammy to arrive, but the minutes ticked by, and still her friend didn't appear – even when their train pulled up at the station platform.

"I can't go to the auditions without Sammy," exclaimed Poppy loyally. "We do everything together."

Mrs Brown was sympathetic but firm. "You must get on the train, Poppy," said the teacher. "You can't miss this opportunity."

Reluctantly, Poppy did as she was told.

Sammy and her mum arrived at the station, just in time to see the train pulling out from the platform. Sammy burst into tears of disappointment.

"I might never get a chance like this again," she sobbed. "And what about Poppy? She needs me to help her get ready."

"Don't worry," soothed Sammy's mother. "Now we've got the car started, I can drive you to the audition. There were some directions with the audition letter. Quick, hop in."

Sammy wiped her tear-stained face and jumped in the car. Maybe, just maybe, they could make the audition if they set off right away.

But the journey down the motorway was very slow and they got stuck in traffic. It was a quarter to twelve by the time they pulled into the car park outside the National School of Ballet.

"Even Poppy's audition will be over by now," said Sammy miserably, looking at her watch. "Maybe they'll let me go in after her," she added hopefully.

But, when Sammy asked at the reception desk, she was disappointed.

"I'm afraid not," the lady told her sternly. "The rules clearly state that all applicants MUST arrive on time for their audition."

"But our car broke down," explained Sammy. "It wasn't our fault. Honestly! I just can't miss this audition."

"I am sorry, dear," replied the receptionist, a little more sympathetically, "but Madame Lemage is a very busy lady. I think she has already left for the day."

Just then, Poppy and Mrs Brown walked into the reception area.

"Sammy!" cried Poppy excitedly, throwing her arms around her friend. "Thank goodness you made it! I got through the audition! What about you, did you manage to get a later audition?"

Fighting to hold back her tears, Sammy explained to Poppy what had happened. "I guess I'll have to try again next year," she told Mrs Brown. "Well done for getting through, Poppy," she added generously, giving her friend a huge hug. "Come on – I'll help you get changed. You can tell me all about it."

In the changing rooms, Sammy helped her friend take down her chignon, and brushed out the hairspray, while Poppy took off her make-up.

"You look great," said Sammy, admiring Poppy's pretty pink leotard and wrap. "I never even got the chance to wear mine." Sadly, Sammy opened her travel case and took out her new ballet shoes and lilac leotard. "I was so looking forward to wearing these and dancing in the salon," she sighed. "They say it's magnificent."

"It is," said Poppy, smiling dreamily.

"I felt just like a real ballerina." Then she had an idea. "You could dance in the salon now," she suggested. "No one would know. Everyone has gone home, so the audition salon will be empty. Then at least you could say you danced at the National School of Ballet."

Sammy stared at her friend. Dare she do as Poppy suggested? Surely there couldn't be any harm in dancing her audition piece? Everyone had left so she wasn't going to disturb anyone.

"I'll do it," she decided suddenly. "Come on Poppy – help me get ready."

When Sammy was dressed, the two girls crept down the corridor, and gingerly opened the door to the audition salon.

The empty room was flooded with light from the enormous windows on one side, and a vaulted ceiling arched over the polished wooden floor.

"OH!" gasped Sammy, gazing at the huge mirrors lining the walls. "It's amazing. I could dance forever in a room like this."

Poppy smiled. "Well, you've only got five minutes, so you'd better make the most of it. Are you ready?"

Quickly, she put Sammy's music for her audition piece on the CD player in the corner and pressed the button.

Sammy shut her eyes as the music

drifted across the salon. Then she began to dance her audition piece.

There was something magical about dancing in such a special place. Sammy felt her body taken over by the music. She felt as light as a feather as she moved around the floor, swirling and pirouetting to the beautiful tune. Never before had she danced so lightly, or so expressively.

Poppy watched in awe. "Sammy really has turned into a butterfly," she whispered. "I've never seen her dance better."

When the music finally ended, Sammy was suddenly brought back down to earth by the sound of clapping. She opened her eyes with a start, and turned to curtsy to Poppy. But it wasn't Poppy who was applauding.

There in the doorway of the salon was an elegant lady with silver hair. She had the unmistakable posture of a dancer.

"Madame Lemage!" gasped Poppy in horror.

Sammy blushed crimson. "I'm really sorry…" she began, mortified to have been discovered by the famous prima ballerina.

"I just…"

But Madame Lemage held up her hand for silence. Then she smiled calmly.

"I came back for my gloves, then I heard music in the salon," she said, fixing Sammy with her clear eyes. "So I came to look for the intruder – but instead I find… a beautiful butterfly. Why did I not see you at the auditions, my dear? You are very gifted."

Sammy blushed crimson again, but this time with pleasure.

"Thank you, Madame," she said, hardly able to believe she was talking with the world-famous Madame Lemage. "It's a rather long story…"

Sammy began to explain what had happened, while Madame Lemage listened patiently.

"So, you see, I had to dance in the salon just once," finished Sammy. "I might never get another chance."

Madame Lemage looked serious.

"Oh, yes you will," she said firmly. "I think that we'll just have to call this a late audition."

"Does that mean what I think it means?" cried Sammy, hardly daring to hope.

"Yes, it does," nodded Madame Lemage, smiling. "I am awarding you a place here, at the National

School of Ballet."

Sammy couldn't believe it, her dream had come true!

"Now it's time to go home, the whole building will be locked up soon. There will be plenty of time for you to enjoy this room in the future and, by the look of your dancing, audiences will be enjoying your performances for many years to come. Oh...and Sammy..." Madame Lemage added. "next time...don't be late!"

Lottie Saves the Day

Lottie Smith was tying up her ballet shoes when she spotted a strange man going into Miss Morgan's office. He was dressed in a suit and had a clipboard in his hand.

"Please, Miss," shouted Lottie, sticking her hand in the air. "There's a man going into your office."

"I know," said Miss Morgan. "Now carry on with your ballet exercises and mind your own business."

"But, Miss," continued Lottie, "he looks pretty shifty. He's got a clipboard and a moustache."

"Sshh," hissed Miss Morgan. "He's not shifty. He's called Mr Cox. He's a very important man from the council, and he's inspecting the ballet school."

"Will he want to inspect me?" asked Lottie. "I can show him my pirouette, if you like." Lottie spun around quickly to show Miss Morgan just how good she was at pirouetting.

"No, thank you," laughed Miss Morgan. "He's not here to inspect you. He's here to inspect the building."

Ballet class was soon over and Lottie forgot all about the man as she waved goodbye to Miss Morgan and climbed into her mum's car. "See you next week," she shouted to her best friend, Becky, through the car window.

The week passed quickly and, on the following Saturday, Lottie's mum pulled up in front of Wilby Ballet School with plenty of time to spare.

"Look, we're the first here," shouted

Lottie, leaping out of the car and running up to the school. As usual, she threw herself against the door, but this time it didn't swing open. "Ouch!" yelped Lottie. "Somebody's locked it. Miss Morgan, let me in!" Lottie hammered on the door with her fist but there was no reply.

"Hang on a minute," called Lottie's mum. "There's a notice on the door. What does it say?"

Lottie stood back and read the notice out loud,

"Wilby Ballet School will be closed until further notice. By order of Wilby County Council."

Just then, Miss Morgan drove into the car park. "I was hoping I would catch you," she called to Lottie and her mum. "I've been trying to phone you all week to tell you about the school being closed down. I managed to speak to everyone else but I couldn't get hold of you."

"We've been out a lot this week," explained Mrs Smith.

"But why has it been closed down?" interrupted Lottie. "Is it because we're no good? We might not be great but we all try our best and we all love your class."

"It's nothing to do with you or any of the other pupils," explained Miss Morgan. "The man from the council discovered that there is a hole in the roof. It looks like it's about to fall in and there's no money to repair it. I'm afraid that you and all the other girls and boys are going to have to find a new ballet school."

"But we don't want to find a new ballet school. We love this one. Besides, what's going to happen to you, Miss?" exclaimed Lottie.

"Well, I suppose I'll have to find a new job. But don't worry about me. Just make sure that you carry on with your ballet. You're very good, you know."

Lottie blushed with pleasure. But then she remembered that the ballet school was going to close down and she began to frown. She was still frowning a few hours later when she was eating her lunch.

"Stop frowning," quipped her dad. "The wind will change direction and your face will stay that way."

"I'm thinking," said Lottie, as she speared a runner bean with her fork and shovelled it into her mouth. She looked really thoughtful as she chewed the bean round and round in her mouth. Then she stopped frowning and swallowed the bean with a gulp. "I know," she cried. "We'll raise lots of money and get the roof mended. Then the ballet school will reopen and everything will be all right."

"Great idea, poppet," smiled Dad, ruffling Lottie's hair. "But raising money takes lots of hard work and lots of organization."

"I know that," cried Lottie. "I know all about fundraising. We can hold a jumble sale, have a sponsored walk and…and…" Lottie quickly tried to think of more ideas. "Oh, I know!" she shouted, slapping her forehead triumphantly. "We can have a huge Ballet Benefit in the park. Everyone from the ballet school can dance and people will pay to watch us. It will be brilliant. We can practise in the garage. You don't mind, do you, Dad?" But she didn't wait for an answer as she pirouetted out of the room.

Mum and Dad were still shaking their heads in bewilderment, when Lottie poked her head back around the door. "Is it okay if I make a few calls?" she asked.

"Of course," said Mum. And, within seconds, Lottie was dialling Becky's telephone number.

The next day, a group of girls and boys gathered in Lottie's bedroom. When they had all found a place to sit, Lottie stood up and looked very serious.

"I think you know why you're all here," she began. "We need to raise some money to mend the ballet school roof. If we don't, we'll have to go to Hislup Dancing Academy, and everyone knows that it's nowhere near as good as our Wilby Ballet School."

"And the girls and boys there are really snooty," volunteered a small boy called Jack.

Everyone nodded their heads in agreement.

Once everyone had quietened down, Lottie told them her ideas for raising money. Everyone agreed that the jumble sale was a good idea, the sponsored walk was a great idea, and the Ballet Benefit was a brilliant idea.

Rachel Moore, who liked reading stories, suggested they dance the tale of Cinderella. Lottie and the other girls and boys thought that sounded good and they quickly agreed who should play who.

Of course, it was decided that Lottie would make a great Cinderella, and Lottie was more than happy to be the star of the show. Then Lottie rang Miss Morgan and told her their idea.

"Well, it's worth a try, count me in!" declared the delighted ballet teacher.

The following Saturday, Lottie and her friends held a jumble sale on the village green. During the week they had gone from door to door collecting people's unwanted things so they could sell them.

That morning, they set it out neatly on tables, and waited for customers to arrive. At first everything went well, with people snapping up bargains, and squabbling over woollies, but then it started to rain and people began to leave. When thunder rumbled in the distance, the pupils of Wilby Ballet School decided to call it a day and packed up early. They didn't make very much money and there were lots and lots of clothes left unsold.

The week after that was the sponsored walk. Mr and Mrs Smith led the children on a trek around the lake. It was a lovely day and everything would have been just perfect if Jack hadn't tripped in a rabbit hole and twisted his ankle. But he did and everyone had to give up half-way round.

"I suppose it's only fair that we only collect half the money," Lottie told the other children, as they waited outside the doctor's surgery. So, what with the jumble sale being washed out and only being able to collect half the sponsored walk money, their money-raising efforts weren't going very well. But they still had the Ballet Benefit to look forward to.

They'd been practising in Lottie's garage for two weeks. Miss Morgan had been helping them and everyone knew exactly what to do. Mrs Smith had even made some wonderful costumes from the clothes left over from the jumble sale. Poor old Jack wouldn't be able to perform because his ankle was bandaged. But he didn't really mind because Lottie told him that he could take the money on the door and count it all up afterwards.

On the night of the Ballet Benefit, the children arrived at the park early. They chattered and giggled as they crowded behind the huge screen that Mr Smith had put up for them to use as a dressing room. Miss Morgan, who was directing the show, handed out costumes and put make-up on the children's excited faces. But she wasn't really in charge. Lottie was.

"Is everyone ready?" Lottie shouted bossily. "We've got five minutes before the curtain goes up."

Five minutes later, the curtain was

raised and Lottie stood on one leg and arabesqued onto the stage. Immediately, the noisy audience fell silent. They remained silent throughout the whole performance. Everyone was spellbound as the pupils of Wilby Ballet School danced beautifully beneath the light of the full moon and starry sky.

Every little girl and boy remembered their dance steps, and nearly everyone remembered their words. As Cinderella was swept away by her Prince Charming, the audience rose to their feet and began to clap madly.

"Bravo! Bravo!" they cried. And, when the children went out to bow, somebody even threw some roses onto the stage. Lottie picked one up and felt like a real prima ballerina. The shouting and clapping didn't stop until Lottie and her friends had returned to bow for the third time.

They were still clapping as all the children gathered behind the dressing-room screen. Miss Morgan had a big smile on her face. She was delighted. "You were all brilliant," she cried. "And the audience loved you."

Lottie and her friends giggled and hugged each other with joy. They'd had a great time and they knew that everything was going to be all right. But they stopped giggling when Jack came in. He held a calculator in one hand and a bag of money in the other, and he wasn't looking at all pleased with himself.

"Err…I'm sorry," he interrupted, "but I've got some bad news. We've only raised £105.93. It's not nearly enough to mend the ballet school roof."

"But what about all the money we raised at the jumble sale and on the sponsored walk? Don't forget that," cried Lottie.

"I haven't," said Jack. "£105.93 is everything added together. That's the lot, I'm afraid."

Lottie slumped down on the grass and put her head in her hands. "Well, that's it then," she groaned. "We've tried our best, but it will be years before we raise enough money. I'm really sorry everyone. Sorry Miss Morgan."

Miss Morgan sat down beside Lottie

and put an arm around her shoulder.

"Don't be sorry," she said. "You all tried your best."

Everyone looked sad as they realized that their dream was over.

Then, suddenly, there was a polite cough and a man poked his head around the screen. "Do you mind if I come in?" he asked. Lottie couldn't believe her eyes. It was Mr Cox, the very important man from the council. She was about to tell him to push off, when Miss Morgan waved him in.

Mr Cox smiled at everyone as they made a gap for him. His smile began to falter when he saw how miserable everyone looked. "I've come to say something," said Mr Cox. "But it looks like I've come at a bad time. Has something terrible happened?"

"YES, IT HAS," shouted Lottie, jumping to her feet. "You closed down our ballet school and it looks like we're never going to be able to raise enough money to save it."

Lottie's parents looked horrified. "Now, Lottie, you shouldn't really talk to Mr Cox like…" began her dad, but Mr Cox waved at him to be quiet.

"I can understand why your daughter and her friends are so angry. I didn't want to close down the ballet school but the roof really is very dangerous. However, now I have seen you all dance, I realize how important it is that the school remains open and I have decided to give you a grant to get the roof fixed." He pushed a hand into the inside pocket of his suit and whipped out a piece of paper just like a magician.

He handed the paper to Miss Morgan.

"Thank you," said Miss Morgan.

"Simply fill in the form and send it to me at the Town Hall and I will get it approved by the end of the week. The Wilby Ballet School should be reopened within the month," he smiled.

Lottie couldn't believe her ears. Mr Cox wasn't such a bad man, after all. She ran over and flung her arms around him. Then a crowd of boys and girls swarmed around him to give him a group hug.

"Thank you, thank you, thank you," they all cried.

"Yes, thank you. Thank you for saving the ballet school," added Miss Morgan, as she rushed forward to hug him too.

"That's okay," Mr Cox beamed. "You know, my job has never been so much fun!"

The Little Swan

This is a story about a little girl called Josie who wanted to be a ballerina.

Even when Josie was very little, if she heard music playing on the radio, or on the television, she would stop whatever she was doing, put her arms above her head, point her toes, and spin and twirl around the room until she was so dizzy she could spin and twirl no longer.

Josie had her first proper ballet shoes when she was three years old. They were so small a mouse could have used them for a sleeping bag. When she grew too big for them Mum hung them on a special hook in Josie's bedroom. There are now six pairs of ballet shoes hanging on the hook, all different sizes, and all made of pink satin.

Josie loved her ballet class. When she started she found it hard to remember the French names for the different steps and positions. They were also hard for her to do, but Josie practised and practised. Her teacher said she had a natural grace and it wasn't long before she was one of the best pupils in her class.

"You take after your Great Aunt Helena," Josie's mum told her one day when she picked her up from class.

Josie knew about Great Aunt Helena. She was born in Russia and had danced with one of the most famous ballet companies in the world. Josie had a picture of her hanging on her bedroom wall. The picture had been taken during a performance of *Swan Lake* and her Great Aunt was holding out her arms and curtsying to the audience. She was so beautiful and so graceful, Josie wanted to be like her more than anything else in the world.

One day, Josie's ballet teacher, Miss Pamela, told them that the school was going to put on a production of *Swan Lake* at the local theatre. The older pupils were to play the more difficult roles but she asked Josie if she would dance the lead swan in the chorus.

"It's a part that's usually played by an older girl," said Miss Pamela, "but you have worked so hard Josie, and your dancing is so good, I think you could do it very well. What do you think? Would you like to give it a try?"

A smile had appeared on Josie's face that was growing bigger by the second.

"I'd love to Miss Pamela!" she cried happily.

"It will take a lot of hard work, but I

know you'll make a lovely swan," Miss Pamela told Josie.

"I love dancing so much it doesn't feel like hard work to me," said Josie.

"Good," said Miss Pamela. "We have two months before the first performance and there will be three rehearsals a week. I know you'll make me proud."

"I will, Miss Pamela," answered Josie, still smiling.

When the two months came to an end, Josie knew the role of the lead swan back to front and she hadn't missed a single rehearsal. She had a new white tutu, white silk tights, new pink satin shoes tied with a pink ribbon and a headdress made of white swan's feathers. She tried on her costume the night before the first performance and stood in front of the picture of her Great Aunt Helena.

"Wish me luck," she whispered.

Her Great Aunt seemed to look down on her with a sweet and serene expression. Josie looked again at the graceful curve of the outstretched arms and the tilt of the lovely head and hoped that one day she would be as good as her. She couldn't wait for tomorrow night's performance to begin.

The next evening, when the curtain went up, Josie was waiting to go on at the side of the stage. She watched intently as the two principal dancers danced a duet together. The music was beautiful and sad and they danced together in perfect unison. Josie was feeling really excited. This was the first time she had danced in public and she wanted so much for it to go well.

The duet finished and the audience cheered loudly. Miss Pamela had told Josie to wait for the clapping to die down so she could hear when the music started again, this way she would be sure of the exact moment when she was to dance onto the stage leading the chorus of little swans behind her.

The cheering stopped at last. Josie held her breath and waited for the music to begin. There was a hush in the audience. The conductor lifted his hand, and the violins began to play. Josie linked arms with the little swan next to her, lifted her chin and began to dance.

When she reached the centre of the stage and saw all the faces in the audience looking up at her, Josie suddenly felt afraid. Her whole body stiffened and her legs felt like jelly. She forced herself to dance on, but her movements were awkward and she felt as if she was frozen to the spot.

"Something's wrong," whispered her mum anxiously from where she was sitting in the front row.

"Is she ill?" Josie's dad asked. But poor Josie wasn't ill. She had stage fright.

As she looked at all the people in the audience she forgot what she was meant to be doing. Josie hadn't felt at all nervous before she went on stage and she had had no idea this was going to happen to her.

Josie's friend Izzy was one of the swans dancing in the chorus. Luckily, she had noticed Josie had stage fright and took the lead, dancing off the stage with the rest of the swans and Josie. When Josie came off stage and saw Miss Pamela's face she burst into tears.

"I couldn't dance," she sobbed, "and I don't know why."

Miss Pamela and Izzy comforted her.

"You had an attack of stage fright, Josie," said Miss Pamela. "It happens to some of the best performers. Don't worry. It will go away, you'll be all right after the interval, you'll see."

But Josie wasn't all right. When she thought about going on again and dancing in front of all those people, she just couldn't do it. Her legs trembled so much she couldn't even put one foot in front of the other for fear of falling over.

During the second part of the performance, an older girl who had danced before in public took Josie's place. Her name was Anna. She danced well and, as Anna made her curtsy to the audience, Josie felt sadder than she had ever felt in her life. The crowd were cheering and clapping and shouting "Bravo!".

"If only it was me out there," Josie thought sadly. "If only they were shouting, 'Bravo!' to me." Later that night, in her bedroom, Josie could hardly bare to look at the picture of her Great Aunt Helena. She felt that she had let her, and everyone else down.

Miss Pamela tried to persuade Josie to dance the following evening, but Josie was still too nervous. Anna took her place and, again, Josie watched miserably from the side of the stage.

The next day was warm and sunny and Mum suggested a walk in the park.

"It will take your mind off things," she said to Josie.

In the middle of the park was a lake where Josie had always loved feeding the swans. She had brought some bread with her and, as she stood at the water's edge, she noticed that the adult swans had a little swan with them.

The little swan was nothing like its parents. The adults had smooth, white feathers and moved with an easy, silent grace, making hardly any ripples in the water. The little swan was covered in straggly brown-grey fluff and he flapped and splashed and churned up the water until it looked like waves on the sea.

Josie watched as the parents tried to teach the young swan how to fly. They showed him how to flap his wings and run across the top of the water before taking off.

"Do you think he'll be able to do it first time?" Josie asked her mum.

"I don't know," replied Mum. "Let's wait and see, shall we?"

They watched, fascinated, as the little swan tried to fly. At first, he simply couldn't manage it. He flapped and flapped his wings but he wasn't able to get out of the water. Then, after a while he managed to lift himself a little way into the air before falling back down again. He did this several times, getting soaked in the process.

Josie watched as he landed in the water for about the tenth time and then turned himself around for another try.

"Come on, little swan," she called to him. "You can do it. I know you can."

As if he had heard her, the tired little

swan flapped his wings again, harder this time, making them do a few extra flaps for good luck. Then he ran a few steps across the top of the water and took off into the air.

"Well done!' shouted Josie.

"Bravo!" shouted Mum.

For a moment Josie forgot she was at the side of the lake on a sunny afternoon watching a little swan learn to fly. In her mind she was back in the theatre listening to the audience as they cheered each night at the end of the ballet. Then she heard Mum's voice.

"Wow, that was brilliant, wasn't it, Josie?" she said. "It's amazing what you can do when you put your mind to it."

Saturday came and it was the last performance of *Swan Lake*. Josie arrived early at the theatre. When Miss Pamela saw her she took her to one side.

"I'm glad to see you, Josie," she said. "This morning Anna stumbled during rehearsal and sprained her ankle. Do you think you can dance the lead swan in the ballet tonight?"

For a moment, Josie couldn't speak. She felt the nervous flutters in her stomach return and she swallowed hard. Then, the picture of the little swan came into her mind. He had been so brave and determined. Surely, if a bird could achieve so much, she could do the same.

Miss Pamela watched her closely.

"What do you think, Josie," she repeated, "will you give it another try?"

"Yes, I'll dance in the ballet tonight,"

Josie smiled.

That night, when Josie was waiting in the wings with all the other little swans, she kept in her mind the image of the real swan on the lake. She remembered how wonderful it had felt when he finally succeeded. She watched the principal dancers perform their duet, and waited for the applause to die down. She saw the conductor lift his hand and heard the orchestra begin to play.

"Now, Josie," she heard Miss Pamela whisper. And, linking arms with the little swan next to her, she lifted her leg, pointed her toe and moved lightly and gracefully onto the centre of the stage.

This time Josie danced beautifully. If she did feel a few butterflies in her tummy, she didn't let them get the better of her. The rest of the chorus followed her example and they all danced better than they had ever done before. When the dance came to an end they moved to the front of the stage to make their curtsies. The audience went wild, clapping and cheering and stamping their feet. It felt amazing, and for the first time Josie knew exactly how the little swan must have felt when he lifted himself above the water and flew around the lake.

That night in bed, Josie was still excited from the show. She turned her head to look at the picture of Great Aunt Helena. Surely the face in the picture was smiling at her.

"I did well tonight, didn't I?" Josie asked the famous ballerina.

And, for a split second, Josie thought she saw her Great Aunt Helena wink at her.

Pink
Ribbons

Katie Price had wanted to be a ballerina for as long as she could remember. She started ballet classes at Miss Pepper's School of Dance when she was just five years old, along with her best friend, Mia.

Mia had stopped going to ballet when she was nine – she preferred riding her pony, Lucan – but Katie loved it. She practised hard, passed her ballet exams and then, when she was 11, she got a place at Madame Rosa's Central Ballet School in the city. It was a dream come true!

"So, you actually have to sleep there too?" asked Mia, as she sprawled on Katie's bed, watching her friend pack her suitcase.

"Just during the week," replied Katie. "I'll come home most weekends."

"But why? I don't understand," cried Mia, who was sad at the thought of not seeing her friend everyday at school.

"Well, this is where I'll have ballet lessons every morning and school work in the afternoons, and the train journey is two hours each way," Katie explained. "Most of the pupils board there."

"But won't you be really nervous and homesick?" asked Mia. "I know I would. I'd be pony-sick for Lucan!"

Katie laughed. "Well, yes, I am nervous," she admitted, "but I'm really excited too. It's what I've always wanted – you know that."

"I know, but I'll miss you so much," said Mia, jumping off the bed and giving Katie a big hug.

"I'll miss you too," said Katie, hugging

her friend right back. "But I'll see you every weekend when I'm home, and we can speak on the phone."

Katie's mother drove Katie to her new ballet school the following morning.

"I'll come and pick you up on Friday evening," said Mum anxiously. "Are you sure you'll be all right?"

"Don't worry," said Katie. "I'll be fine."

And Katie was fine – at least at first. She loved the ballet school's light, airy practice studios with their huge mirrored walls. She loved her pretty bedroom, which she shared with two other new pupils, Yoshiko and Chloe. And she loved being able to dance every single day.

At the end of the first week, the new students had a lesson with the famous Madame Rosa herself.

"I've heard she's strict," whispered Chloe, as she put on her ballet shoes.

Yoshiko was warming up at the barre. "Yes," she agreed. "One of the older girls said that if you don't get something right, she shouts at you!"

"But she was really nice at the auditions," said Katie.

"Well, we'll soon find out," muttered Chloe. "Here she comes!"

The door opened and Madame Rosa walked into the room. She stood in front of them, leaning slightly on her black walking stick, which had a large silver ball at the top for a handle. Her dark hair, streaked with white, was scraped back in a bun at the nape of her neck. As always, she was wearing a black leotard, a long skirt and black tights. Over her shoulders was a long, fringed shawl, patterned with red roses.

Madame Rosa looked at each of the girls in turn. Her sharp brown eyes seemed to see right into them, as if she could read their innermost thoughts.

"Bonjour, mes filles," she said finally, in a heavy French accent. "Good morning, girls!"

"Good morning, Madame Rosa," chorused the students.

"Now, you are here at my ballet school because you are good dancers, this we know. Some of you may even join a ballet company one day. But, I must tell you now," she continued sternly, "the road ahead is hard. You must have patience. You must have perseverance. And you must practise, practise, practise." At the repetition of each word, Madame Rosa thumped the floor with her stick.

"Now, to work!" she exclaimed. "Right hand on the barre! Plié! Plié in first position…in second position…now in third…Good! Now, fourth…and fifth. Now demi-plié, each position! Concentrate! Now, grand plié!"

Along with the rest of the students, Katie bent her knees smoothly and rose up on her toes, working through each step and the five positions of her feet and arms.

Madame Rosa put the girls through their barre exercises for half an hour. Then they moved to the middle of the room for centre work. It was difficult without the support of the barre, but Katie danced well.

Finally, Madame Rosa asked the girls

to put on their pointe shoes with hard blocked toes.

Katie had been dancing en pointe for six months but, during her first lesson with Madame Rosa, she couldn't stop wobbling.

"Katie! Again!" called Madame Rosa. "Preparation for pirouette! From fourth position, if you please!" But it was no good. Katie kept losing her balance. She was in tears of frustration by the end of the lesson.

"Never mind, Katie," said Chloe, putting her arm around Katie's shoulders. "You'll be better next week, you'll see."

But Katie was not better the following week. In fact, if anything, her dancing was much worse.

"Katie! Lift your arm higher," shouted Madame Rosa. "Katie! Turn out your leg more, please!"

The next Friday it was the same. Katie couldn't seem to put a foot right. She began to dread her dance classes with Madame Rosa.

At the weekends when she went home, Katie spent most of the time in her bedroom, feeling miserable. Even Mia and Lucan couldn't cheer her up.

"You are happy at Madame Rosa's, aren't you, Katie?" asked her mum.

"Oh, fine!" Katie fibbed. "I'm just tired, that's all."

"I don't understand, Katie," said Madame Rosa one Friday morning. "You were such a good dancer at the audition...maybe we were wrong about you. Maybe your feet aren't strong enough for pointe work..."

"I think it's my shoes," said Katie desperately. "Maybe my shoes don't fit properly!"

"Show me," demanded Madame Rosa. Katie took off her shoes and handed them to Madame Rosa.

"Mmmm," said Madame Rosa. "They don't look worn to me…and a good dancer never blames her shoes," she added. She looked severely at Katie, who blushed scarlet to the tips of her ears.

"Even so," Madame Rosa continued thoughtfully, "a new pair of ribbons could be just what you need…Yes," she said, making up her mind. "There's a ballet shop just around the corner, on Victoria Street. Ask the lady for some new ribbons, sew them to your shoes, and I'll see you at class next week."

Fighting back tears, Katie grabbed her things and raced out of the studio.

Victoria Street was a quiet little road tucked behind the ballet school. Katie had never been there before. She walked past a row of old-fashioned shops with small, bow-fronted windows. The ballet shop, called Pink Ribbons, was on a corner.

A bell jangled as Katie pushed open the door. It had been bright outside but, once Katie's eyes had adjusted to the shop's dim light, she looked around, enchanted. "Oh," she breathed. "What a magical place!"

The shop was packed with all kinds of dancewear, from tights and tutus to leg warmers and leotards. Behind the wooden counter were rows and rows of glass-fronted drawers filled with ballet shoes. The walls were covered with posters of old ballet performances. Katie's glance fell on a photograph of a graceful ballerina dancing the part of the swan in *Swan Lake*.

She sighed, her eyes filling with tears. She'd never be good enough to be a great ballerina like the one in the picture.

"Can I help you, dear?"

A kind-looking old lady was standing behind the counter.

"Oh, yes, please," said Katie. "I've come for some ribbons for my ballet shoes. Madame Rosa sent me."

"Madame Rosa?" asked the old lady.

Katie nodded.

"Well now, let me see…" said the old lady, opening one of the drawers behind her. "Are you happy at the dance school, dear?" she asked.

"Oh yes, I am," said Katie. "I mean…I was," she stammered, and then, unable to hold back her tears any longer, she began to cry.

"There, there," said the old lady, going over to Katie. "Take my handkerchief, then

sit down and tell me all about it."

The old lady had such a kind voice, Katie found herself telling her about the problems she had been having at Madame Rosa's Central Ballet School.

"It seemed so easy at Miss Pepper's," sobbed Katie. "At Madame Rosa's, everyone is a much better dancer than me. I can't seem to dance any more – even simple steps!"

"Dry your eyes," said the old lady, "and cheer up! I think I've got just the thing you need — some special pink ribbons, magic ribbons, to sew onto your shoes."

She disappeared into the back of the shop. "Yes, here they are," she said, coming back, and she put a pair of long, pale pink, satin ribbons into Katie's hand.

"Magic ribbons," breathed Katie, eyes shining. "Really?"

"Yes," said the old lady. "Sew them to your ballet shoes and you will be able to dance well again. Trust me. Will you promise me you'll do that?"

"Yes, I will," promised Katie. "Thank you! Oh, thank you!"

"Go on then, dear," smiled the shopkeeper. "Hurry back to school, and good luck!"

Katie sewed the magic pink ribbons in her shoes that evening, and she wore them to Madame Rosa's ballet class the following week.

She danced beautifully.

"Did you get some new ribbons, Katie?" asked Madame Rosa.

"Yes," replied Katie.

"Well they seem to have worked," declared Madame Rosa. "Well done! Yes, a big improvement!"

Week by week, Katie's dancing got better and better and, as she improved, she became more confident. She even began to look forward to her weekly lesson with Madame Rosa.

"Oh, Mia," she told her friend excitedly over the telephone one evening. "You'll never guess what! Madame Rosa has picked me to dance the lead role in the school's next performance. Will you come and see me dance?"

"Just try and stop me," said Mia. "You

seem much happier now, Katie. I was getting a bit worried about you a few weeks ago."

"Mia, if I tell you something, will you promise me you won't tell anyone?" Katie whispered.

"Cross my heart. What is it?" Mia asked. So Katie told Mia all about Madame Rosa's class, the shopkeeper and the magic pink ribbons. "Magic ribbons?" murmured Mia wonderingly. "I could do with some magic ribbons to weave into Lucan's mane. Then maybe we'd win a rosette at the next gymkhana!"

"Oh, Mia," giggled Katie. "You are so funny!"

Over the next few weeks, the girls at the ballet school practised hard for their performance. Then, on the morning of the show, disaster struck! Katie couldn't find her ballet shoes with the magic pink ribbons anywhere.

"They must be here somewhere," said Chloe, helping Katie search their bedroom. The girls searched high and low but they couldn't find them. "They will turn up, Katie, don't you worry," added Yoshiko. "You've got your spare shoes, haven't you?"

"It's not that," said Katie. "I can only dance in the shoes with the pink ribbons. You don't understand!"

After her lessons, Katie rushed out of school and along Victoria Street to the ballet shop.

"Help me, please," she gasped breathlessly to the old lady. "The ribbons.

The magic ribbons you gave me! I've lost them and I need them tonight, for the performance. I've got the lead role. I have to dance well!"

"Hush! Hush! Calm down! You mustn't worry!" said the old lady.

"But I need them! I really do!" exclaimed Katie.

"No, you don't, my dear. You see the ribbons I gave you were not magic – not magic at all."

"Wh…what do you mean?" stammered Katie who was really confused.

"You just needed confidence, that's all," said the old lady. "The ribbons gave you that, didn't they? You see – the magic was in your feet all along, I could tell!"

She chuckled. "I did the same thing for another young ballerina, many years ago. See, there's her photo on the wall, dancing the lead in *Swan Lake*. It's hard to imagine that she needed a little confidence when she was a young dancer, just starting out like you, but she did."

"Who is it?" breathed Katie. "What's her name?"

"Don't you recognize her?" asked the old woman, smiling. "Why, it's Madame Rosa, your teacher! I suspect she knew just what she was doing when she sent you to my shop for some new ribbons. Now, hurry along, dear, or you'll be late for your performance."

Katie dashed back to the ballet school. As she raced down the corridor towards her room, she ran straight into Madame Rosa.

"Why, Katie, I was coming to find you!" said Madame Rosa. "Why are you rushing so? Is everything all right?"

"It is now," said Katie. "I've been talking to the lady at the ballet shop. She said you got some magic ribbons there too, a long time ago…well, not so long ago," stammered Katie, blushing.

"It's all right, Katie," smiled Madame Rosa, interrupting. "I know what you mean. It is a special shop, isn't it?" she added, eyes twinkling.

"Now, I've found a pair of ballet shoes," she continued. "I believe they are yours?"

"Oh yes," said Katie. "Thank you!"

"All right. Enjoy the performance tonight, Katie. I am sure you will dance beautifully!"

And she did – even though she knew the pink ribbons weren't really magic. The old lady in the ballet shop was right, and everyone in the audience (including Mia and Katie's mum and dad) agreed – the lead ballerina danced so gracefully, she must have had magic in her feet.

The Snow Queen

"Evie! Evie! Look!" called Shelley, in great excitement, as Evie walked through the door of the Darlington Dance Academy for her Saturday morning dance class.

"We're going to be having auditions, real auditions, for the school's Christmas performance! Come and see!"

Evie hurried over to join her friend in front of the notice board. It read:

THE SNOW QUEEN

Auditions will be held on Saturday 15th October at 10.30am. Students will be given the opportunity of auditioning for these roles: • The Snow Queen • Gerda

• Kai • Prince • Princess • Robber Girl •
Flower Witch • Witch of Finland •
Grandmother • Sprites •

We will also be auditioning dancers to take the roles of reindeer, flowers and robbers.

Maria Darlington

Principal, Darlington Dance Academy

"Which part do you want to try for, Evie?" asked Shelley. "I like the sound of the Snow Queen!"

"As long as you don't mind dancing the part of someone EVIL!" hissed Evie, making her hands into claws and pulling an ugly face.

"Aha, I see someone knows the story of the Snow Queen already!" said a voice behind them. It was Miss Darlington, their dance teacher.

"I hope you're both going to try out for

the main parts!" she smiled. "Now, hurry along, it's nearly time for class!"

While they were getting changed, Evie told Shelley the story of the Snow Queen.

"She puts a splinter of ice in Kai's heart and takes him away to her palace in the far North," said Evie. "Gerda, his best friend, goes off to find him. Gerda's grandmother gives her a red rose so she can remember her home and on the way she's helped by a prince and princess – they give her a fur coat and muff to keep her warm."

"What does the Robber Girl do?" interrupted Rebecca, who was listening in. "She sounds fun!"

"Well, at first she wants to steal Gerda's coat and muff but then she takes pity on her and helps her," said Evie.

"And the witches?"

"The Flower Witch seems nice but she enchants Gerda so she forgets her journey

for a while. The Witch of
Finland helps her."

"And does she find
Kai?" Shelley asked.

"Yes, and with
the help of the red
rose, she melts the
ice splinter and
they return home."

"Well, Oliver
will get the part of
Kai," said Rebecca.
"I mean, there are
only three boys in the
whole ballet school and the other two are
too young."

"True, but at least he can dance well!"
laughed Evie.

"There are lots of good dancers," said
Shelley. "It'll be tough to get a good part,
but I'm sure you'll get one, Evie," she

smiled. "Probably Gerda, if you want the main part. You're easily the best dancer."

"Well, I'll try," blushed Evie, "but you must too, Shelley. See if you can get the part of the Snow Queen!"

After class, Evie couldn't wait to rush home and tell her parents all about the auditions.

"But Evie...the 15th of October," said Mum checking the calendar on the wall, "...that's Nan and Grandad's wedding anniversary party. Sorry, but we're away that weekend."

Evie's face crumpled and tears sprung to her eyes.

"But the auditions, Mum! It's not fair! Do I have to go to Nan and Grandad's. I could stay with Shelley, couldn't I?"

"I'm sure you could, Evie, but it's their 50th wedding anniversary. That's really special, you know. They'd be terribly upset if you don't come."

Evie felt tears roll down her cheeks. "Oh, Mum," she sniffed. "I know I should go to Nan and Grandad's party – and I will, but I really wanted to try for the role of Gerda. It's the best part!"

"I know, sweetheart. Look, I can't promise anything, but let me give Miss Darlington a ring and explain."

Mum came back ten minutes later. "It's as I thought. Miss Darlington said she knows you're a good dancer and that you'd have a chance of getting one of the main parts but she can't hold a part open for you. It wouldn't be fair to the others if they auditioned for a role and it went to someone who wasn't there."

"Oh, Mum," sighed Evie. "If only the auditions had been on another day!"

"Yes," agreed Mum, "but I suppose Miss Darlington needs to get the parts sorted out before the half-term holiday. Cheer up, Evie, there'll be other parts and other performances."

At school on Monday, Evie told Shelley that she wouldn't be able to audition.

"Oh no, Evie!" cried Shelley. "But I'm sure Miss Darlington will save you a part – even if it's a small one."

"I hope so," replied Evie sadly, "but I really wanted to try for the part of Gerda…"

The weekend of the 15th October arrived and Evie went with her parents to her grandparents' wedding anniversary party. Everyone had a wonderful time, and Evie loved seeing her grandparents, aunts, uncles and cousins, but she couldn't help wondering how the auditions had gone, and who had got which part.

She couldn't wait any longer to find out, so she phoned Shelley from the party.

"I think I danced well," Shelley

exclaimed. "Rebecca was good too, but we don't know if we've got parts yet. Miss Darlington is going to put up a list on the noticeboard in time for next Saturday's dance class."

Evie went to the dance school early the following Saturday. Miss Darlington had just pinned a notice on the board. Rebecca was to dance the part of Gerda, Shelley had got the part of the Snow Queen and

Oliver was Kai. Evie looked down the list for her own name. Right at the bottom, she found it. She was a flower – a boring, old flower!

"Evie, I'm glad you're here early!" said Miss Darlington. "I want a chat with you."

Evie followed Miss Darlington into her office, trying hard not to show her disappointment.

"Now, Evie," said Miss Darlington, sitting behind her desk. "I know you're bound to be upset that you've only got a small part in this year's Christmas performance, especially as you're one of my best dancers, but I have a proposal for you."

"We've got just two months, Evie, to put on this show," continued Miss Darlington. "As well as teaching all the dancers their parts, there are costumes to make, and props to organize. I need to get Mr Wilson to sort out the lighting, and students from the art college to paint the scenery. I wondered whether you would like to help me. Last year's assistant has since had a baby and won't be able to spare the time. What do you think?"

Evie was silent for a moment. "Yes…I'd like to help," she replied, "but I've never done anything like this before…I mean, I don't know anything about making costumes or…"

"Oh, don't worry. A lot of it is organizing other people to do things," said Miss Darlington, "and I think you'll be good at that. I'm also hoping that you can help with the choreography for the flower dance. That's why I've given you the part of a flower, so you can teach the children from the beginners' class their dance steps and lead them on stage."

"I'd like that," said Evie, smiling. She started to feel better about not getting the part of Gerda. At least she would be involved with the show.

"Good," said Miss Darlington. "Then it's settled."

On Monday evening, Evie began her first job as Miss Darlington's assistant – teaching the beginners' class of over-excited four year olds how to dance like flowers.

"Point your toes and stretch up your arms," called Evie, showing them the dance steps. "Now, try to be graceful like a swan!" There was a lot of giggling and waving of arms in the wrong direction, but Evie was patient and soon they were all dancing beautifully.

In the evenings after school, Evie was busy with all sorts of things. She went to the art college with Miss Darlington to ask the teachers if some of the students could paint the scenery. She also made a list of all the costumes and props they would need for

the performance. She found a fabric red rose for Rebecca to hold as she danced the part of Gerda, and lots of other props, such as a sledge for Kai and a basket for the Flower Witch.

She wrote notes to parents to ask if they could help to make the costumes. She even went to jumble sales and charity shops to look for fabric and was delighted when she found some lovely shiny-white satin material – perfect for the ice sprites' tunics – and a shimmering silver stole that could be made into a cloak for the Snow Queen.

Then there were meetings with Mr Wilson, their lighting expert, where they talked through the ballet and what sort of lighting they needed.

"Could we have a special effect so it looks like snowflakes are falling?" Evie asked Mr Wilson shyly. "We could have it at the end, you know, when Gerda reaches the Snow Queen's palace.

"That's a wonderful idea, Evie!" exclaimed Miss Darlington.

"And easy enough to do," agreed Mr Wilson, smiling.

Every Saturday morning, Evie looked after Miss Darlington's notes while she taught the older dancers their main roles. Soon Evie knew everyone's part and helped Rebecca and Shelley practise their steps over and over again.

Everything was going well until three weeks before the performance when disaster struck! Miss Darlington came down with flu.

"Oh, Evie," she wheezed over the telephone. "We may have to cancel. I don't feel well enough to hold any rehearsals this week, and there's so much to do…"

"Please, don't cancel," said Evie. "Just get well, and don't worry. I'll stand in until you're better – if it doesn't work out, we can always cancel later."

"Well, if you're sure," said Miss Darlington doubtfully.

"Trust me!" said Evie.

For the next week and a half, Evie was like a whirlwind. She stood in for Miss Darlington at all the dance rehearsals and made everyone practise their steps. In the evenings, she telephoned the art college and made sure the scenery was going to be ready in time for the dress rehearsal, she checked that all the costumes were being made and fitted everyone, and she designed the programmes on her computer with her dad's help. She also decorated the entrance hall of the ballet school with a beautiful silver Christmas tree covered with blue tinsel and long white ice crystals.

"You seem to be enjoying all this, Evie," said her mum. "You're working so hard, I'm really proud of you!"

"Thanks, Mum. At first I was really sad I couldn't have a main part, but I've really enjoyed helping Miss Darlington," said Evie. "I still want to be a ballerina one day, because I love dancing more than anything, but if I don't make it, I'd like to work in the theatre. I had no idea there's so much to do behind the scenes!"

Miss Darlington returned to the ballet

school a few days before the dress rehearsal. She was amazed that Evie had managed to keep everything on schedule.

"You're a star, Evie," she exclaimed, "you really are!"

There were lots of problems to sort out at the dress rehearsal. Mrs May, the pianist, left her music at home. Luckily, Evie knew where to find the spare score.

Rebecca lost the red rose, so Evie had to dash out and buy another one. Then one of the sprites ripped her tunic, so Evie had to sew it up.

"Never mind!" said Miss Darlington cheerfully. "Dress rehearsals usually go wrong. It'll be all right on the night!"

And it was!

The curtain came down at the end of the performance to huge applause. All the performers took it in turns to go forward and take a bow. From the wings, Evie clapped along with the audience as they gave Shelley, Rebecca and Oliver an extra round of applause.

Next, one of the youngest ballerinas presented Miss Roberts with a huge bouquet of flowers. Everyone cheered, but Miss Roberts raised her hand and called for quiet.

"Thank you all so much, but you know

it takes lots of people to help make a performance special. You've already thanked the dancers and some of the other people who've helped tonight," she said, smiling at Mrs May and nodding at Mr Wilson and the art students who were sitting in the front row. "But there is someone else here who deserves a special thank you – my assistant, Evie Fitzpatrick!"

"Evie, where are you? Please come up on stage!"

Shelley and Rebecca gave Evie a nudge and she walked onto the stage, blushing, to stand next to Miss Darlington.

"I can truly say that without Evie this performance would never have happened," continued Miss Roberts. "She stood in for me when I was ill. She has been my co-choreographer, my wardrobe mistress, our lighting assistant…you name it, she's done it. Please can everyone give a special round of applause…FOR EVIE!"

One of the little girls who played a flower came on stage and presented Evie with her own bouquet of flowers, and Evie grinned as she got the loudest applause of the evening. She realized that it didn't matter not having a big part – it was definitely the taking part that counts!